ANNA MEETS THE SOCK STEALER

Written by
Peggy Grigowski

Illustrated by
Darren Wheeling

Anna Meets the Sock Stealer
Copyright 2013: Peggy Grigowski
All rights reserved.
Published by Wynwidyn Press, LLC
www.wynwidynpress.com

Softcover ISBN 978-0-9855459-9-4
1st Edition, January 2013
10 9 8 7 6 5 4 3 2 1

Printed in the U.S.A.

Cover and interior illustrations by Darren Wheeling

Interior Layout by Dave Reed

Photography by Lauren Hackworth – www.heirloomsphoto.com

Manufactured by Thomson-Shore, Dexter, MI (USA); RMA100DS402, June, 2013

Thank you, Anthony, for your great imagination. Without it, and the invention of the 'Green Monster' Edgar would have never come to life!

Mom

Chapter
One

_____

Lion and Fizzy's Wedding

Yeah, a party! Anna and Hailie danced around Anna's bedroom as they pulled out the dress-up clothes from Anna's closet. Hailie noticed a pile of mismatched socks in the corner.

"Hey, why did you put your socks in your closet?" Hailie asked then continued, "And why are they all mismatched?"

"What? I didn't, Silly Head. I wonder who did." Anna exclaimed.

Hailie was Anna's best friend and she was visiting Anna's house. Both girls put on some of Anna's mom's and grandma's old dresses, hats, gloves and high heels.

The girls were pretending they were going to a wedding, just like Anna was really going to go to the next day. Anna was excited about the wedding; *she* was the flower girl.

"Being the flower girl is the most important job of all at a wedding," Anna told Hailie

"Why?" asked Hailie. She had never been to a wedding before.

"The flower girl scatters the rose petals for the bride to walk on that leads the way to the groom."

"But aren't the bride and the groom the most important?" asked Hailie.

"No, silly. How could they get married if someone didn't spread the rose petals! You have to have them or there can't be a wedding! That's why I cut these petals out of paper. Even a pretend wedding *has* to have rose petals."

"Oh," said Hailie, shrugging, as she reached for a powder puff. "Puffy puff powder to my nose," she said as she giggled and powdered her nose. Anna used a brush and put sparkly blue eye shadow over both her eyes.

The girls had everything set up in Anna's room. The reception would be in the middle of her room and the wedding would take place in front of her window. The bride and the groom were two of their favorite stuffed animals. The Bride was 'Lion,' a fuzzy stuffed brown and yellow bear and the Groom was 'Fizzy,' a soft, cuddly, big-eyed pink bunny.

Anna dressed Lion in a wedding dress her Grandma Pidgie had made from an old lace curtain. She put the veil on Lion's head and sat the bear a short way away from her window. "Doesn't Lion look pretty, Hailie?"

"She sure does. Isn't Fizzy handsome as the groom?" He had on a paper vest the girls made from construction paper. Hailie set a hat Anna used on snowmen in the winter over one of Fizzy's ears. She set him down right up by the window to wait for Lion to come down the aisle. Hailie had made a 'red carpet' aisle out of an old red towel Anna's mother gave them.

Hailie and Anna set the small table with a tablecloth, dishes, a teapot and a plate of Grandma Pidgie's Amazing Peanut Butter cookies and each had a napkin for their lap. The girls each had two peanut butter cookies and there was one each for the bride and the groom. Anna's grandmother had sent the cookies to Anna earlier in the week. It was so much fun getting a box in the mail, especially from grandma!

Finally, all was ready. "Let the wedding begin!" shouted Anna.

Hailie and Anna had fun. Anna carefully scattered almost all the paper rose petals in her basket as Hailie walked Lion down the aisle. Hailie hummed the wedding song, "Here Comes the Bride"...dee dum dee dum...

I need to make sure I do this right tomorrow, thought Anna as she hummed along with Hailie; *I have the most important job of all.*

She tossed the rest of her flower petals at Hailie as she stood Lion next to her groom.

Anna's stuffed teddy bear married Hailie's floppy-eared big-eyed rabbit. Anna pronounced them Bunny and Bear. Just then, out of the corner of her eye, Anna thought she saw a greenish swish of color run out of her bedroom door.

"Hey! Did you see that?" she shrieked.

"See what?" asked Hailie.

"That green thing!" Anna screeched.

"I didn't see any invisible green thing," Hailie laughed.

Anna shrugged but kept an eye out for the 'green

thing.' She *knew* that she had seen *some*thing.

"Time for the reception," Hailie announced.

They brought Lion and Fizzy to the table and put them in their chairs. Anna and Hailie sat down too and each girl put her napkin in her lap. Anna looked down at her plate. She was a bit puzzled.

"Hailie, did you eat one of my cookies?" Hailie shook her head, giggled and said, "Maybe Lion ate it! We need music!"

Hailie turned on Anna's CD player. They danced with each other and each danced with the bride and the groom. When Anna sat the bear bride and the bunny groom back at the table, she noticed that not only was one cookie missing, but now there was a bite out of Lion's cookie.

"Hailie! Did you eat a bite out of Lion's cookie?" Anna asked.

"What cookie? I ate two already" Hailie said.

"This cookie!" Anna held up the bitten cookie to show Hailie.

"I didn't take a bite out of that cookie!" Hailie scolded.

"Well, who did then?" Anna said with a huffy tone. "It didn't just eat itself!"

"Not me! Maybe Fizzy got hungry," Hailie said with a giggle.

"It's not funny, Hailie!" Anna shouted.

Just then, Anna's mother came in. "It is time for Hailie to go home. Please clean up, now."

Hailie brought the plates and the one bitten cookie and teapot back to the kitchen. Anna put her teddy bear back on her bed and moved her table back by the wall where it belonged. Again, she 'thought' she saw something green flash by her bedroom door. *I must be tired,* she thought.

Anna said goodbye to Hailie and then hurried back to her room. She needed to get her things ready for the wedding before she went to bed.

She and her mother were laying out Anna's clothes for the wedding. She had her pink and white dress with the lace on it hanging on her closet door. The pink ribbons for her hair were on the table and her new white shoes with the pink flowers were on the floor under the table. Anna opened her sock drawer to get out her pink and white socks. It always made a funny noise when she opened it. Her mother said it was because it was an old dresser. Anna reached in to get her socks, but there were only a bunch of odd socks in her drawer. She could only find one of the socks she needed for the wedding! Then she remembered the socks in the corner of her closet.

Anna walked to her closet and pointed at the pile of socks and asked her mom, "Why did you put one of each of my socks in my closet?"

"Don't be silly Anna! Why would I put any socks in your closet and not in your sock drawer?"

"Well, I didn't put them there." Anna replied.

"Oh Anna!" Mom laughed.

Anna bent down and started going through the pile of socks as she looked for her wedding sock.

"Where's my other sock? It's not here. Where is it?"

"Look in your drawer," answered her mother. "I know I put them both in there two days ago."

"I already looked and only found one." Anna replied.

"Well, look again. Maybe you over-looked it." Mom told her then continued;. "Put the socks from the closet in your drawer, too."

Again, Anna looked in her sock drawer for her pretty pink and white sock with lacy ruffles around the top. The sock was not in the drawer. She matched up her yellow sock with the one from the closet. She matched up her two purple socks with the white unicorns. She put the one red sock with the purple stripe with the other one and folded them together. She put the two blue socks with the light blue polka-dots together and was left with just one orange sock. One orange sock? *I know they were both here this morning,* thought Anna, *because I almost wore them instead of my flowered ones!*

"It isn't here, Mom. I triple looked!"

Is it under the bed? Anna wondered. Is it in my toy box? Is it in my closet?

Anna searched her bedroom for the sock. She looked under her pillows, beneath her blankets, in her dollhouse, and in her cat, Willie's bed. She even checked to see if he was wearing it.

Anna needed that sock. They were the socks for the wedding and they matched her dress. How could she do her important job with only one sock? Anna could not find her sock anywhere. Where could it have gone?

"Mom! Mom!" she shouted. "Could you please help me find my sock? I can't find it anywhere. Oh no! What am I going to do?" Anna whimpered.

"Have you looked in the living room?" her mom asked.

Anna ran into the living room and looked under

the sofa. Her sock was not there, but she did find her favorite book. She looked on the chair, in the chair, and under the chair, but still no sock!

Maybe it was in the kitchen. Anna looked in the cupboards, in the broom closet, and under the table. No sock! Her sock was nowhere to be found. But she did find Willie's squeaky toy mouse.

"Anna," her mom exclaimed, "Why do you always lose just one sock? Where do they all go? What could be happening to all of your socks? Check in the dryer!"

Anna looked inside the dryer. She looked behind it. Then she got up on her tip-toes and peeked inside the washer. No sock, but she did find one of her hair ribbons. Still no socks!

That night, Anna lay in bed thinking about the disappearance of her socks. Where do they go? She wondered if they would mysteriously re-appear just as they had strangely disappeared. Her mother had said she could wear her white tights instead, but she didn't want to wear her tights, she wanted her pretty new socks!

She also thought about the disappearing cookie and the green flash she thought she'd seen. She knew she hadn't eaten either one of her cookies and she also knew she did not take a bite out of Lion's. She was pretty sure Hailie must have eaten it. Very strange, she thought. With thoughts of socks, cookies and green flashes coming and going, Anna finally drifted off to sleep.

Chapter
Two

A
Sock Stealer?

As Anna lay sleeping, a creaking sound awakened her. She listened. There was a creaking sound at her dresser where the drawer always stuck a little. She pulled the covers close up around her neck, gripping them tightly and scrunching her eyes closed. She heard the noise again and squeezed the covers tighter. Anna was scared, but she wanted to know what the noise was so she slowly un-scrunched one eye to see, as she gripped the covers tighter.

Then she saw it! There was a little chubby monster with long legs and peculiar ears standing beside her dresser. He had a long, long tail with a puffball on the end of it. She kept one eye opened watching this weird creature in her room. He reached into her sock drawer and took out one of her yellow socks. Then he took one of her unicorn socks! He was the one 'stealing' her socks.

Anna leapt out of bed and ran over to the strange creature. He was so startled that he dropped all the socks he was holding.

"Who are you? Why are you stealing my socks?" Anna demanded.

The creature looked at Anna and said in a quivering voice, "My name is Edgar. I am a Fuzzawalla from a far away planet." He took several steps back from Anna. She was standing there in her pajamas with her hands on her hips looking very ferocious.

"You're a fuzzy what?" Anna said with a huffy tone.

Then he continued, "A Fuzzawalla and I'm sorry I
scared you. I didn't mean to wake you up. I just wanted

to steal some socks, but I promise I will return them soon."

Anna stared at the strange green creature who was in her bedroom." Why are you stealing my socks, Edgar, from some far away planet?" Anna demanded.

"Well, I, I um, well I like wearing cool, mismatched socks. So I come to Earth through a Magic Red Rock, 'steal' some socks and then in a week or two, I return the socks to where I stole them from," Edgar replied.

"Return them?" Anna said, and then continued, "You mean you trade them for different ones when you return them, right?"

Edgar nodded his head up and down for yes with a smile.

Anna looked down at Edgar's feet. There was her sock, right there, on his left foot and a different one on his right!

Anna squealed. "That's my sock!" she said pointing to Edgar's foot. "I need that sock to wear to a wedding tomorrow. I'm the flower girl and that is the most important job at a wedding, you know."

"Ohhh dear!" Edgar said, "Here, you can have it back." He quickly reached down and took the sock off and handed it back to Anna. She was scary and much bigger than he was.

"Where's my other orange sock?" demanded Anna. "I can't find it. I bet you stole that one too."

Edgar looked puzzled. He scratched his head. He scratched his long tail. "I didn't steal your orange sock."

Anna glared at Edgar. "You stole my pink and white wedding sock. I think you took—"

Right at that moment, a bright red light shone through Anna's bedroom window. It was so bright that Anna ran to her window to see what it was. Edgar ran to the window too.

"That's my Magic Red Rock," Edgar said. He pointed up to the sky at a red colored bright star. "That's my home. I live way up there." It was very far away out there amongst the stars.

Anna looked at Edgar and asked, "Are there more Fuzzy whats?"

"Oh, yes, many Fuzzawallas!" exclaimed Edgar with excitement.

Anna and Edgar were standing by Anna's window, looking out at the glowing red rock.

"I have to go home now," explained Edgar. "Can I steal some socks for us to use? I promise I'll bring them back next week." Anna stood there with her hands on her hips and looked down at Edgar.

"No! You cannot steal my socks. And it is 'May I' not 'Can I?' It is obvious you can steal them since you have been! But you didn't ask!" she huffed. "You need to ask if you want to borrow something, it is wrong to just take it when you didn't pay for it!"

Edgar stood there looking at his sockless feet. He looked very sad.

"Stealing is bad, Edgar and will get you into trouble. You must ask someone first to use, borrow or have something and if they let you, only then is it okay. Otherwise it is very naughty!"

Edgar thought about what Anna had just told him. "May I borrow some socks?" he asked. "Not your pretty pink one, of course. What is a wedding?

"You may borrow my yellow sock. A wedding is when two people get married."

"What's married?" he asked.

Anna shook her head. Edgar from a far away red planet didn't know much about life on Earth. "Grown-up people get married when they love each other. A flower girl spreads rose petals on the ground for them to walk on and then they are married." Anna took her yellow sock out of her drawer and handed it to Edgar.

He smiled and his long tail started bobbing and swirling.

Anna thought *if all the Fuzzawallas are as small as Edgar is, I could give them my old socks I have outgrown and don't use anymore. Well, I could if he hadn't taken them already!*

Anna looked in her drawer. "I like all these socks," she said. "Don't take any of these." She looked on the shelf in her closet. In a box marked 'Old Socks' she found some socks that didn't fit any more. Soon she had a small basket full of socks. She smiled and offered it to Edgar. "Here, you can take all these socks home for you and your friends."

Edgar took the basket and smiling said, "Thank you, Anna."

"I'll leave my old socks in a box in my closet just for you so that next time you want socks, you will know where to look."

"I like that idea, said Edgar. "That sock drawer sticks and makes a lot of noise. I remember coming here a long time ago, but I picked other houses because I don't like that squeaky-noisy drawer. I just started coming back to your house to find socks, but that drawer still squeeks! That is why last time I was here I put some socks in your closet."

The Magic Red Rock began glowing even brighter. Edgar jumped up and grabbed the basket of socks, said thank you, and ran out to the backyard where the Magic Red Rock was. Anna followed Edgar and watched as he jumped into the Magic Red Rock and disappeared.

Just as quickly as the Magic Red Rock had opened and Edgar jumped in, it closed and shrunk into a small little sparkling red rock.

Anna stood there looking puzzled for a second, and then she reached down and picked up the Magic Red Rock and went back inside. Anna was happy that she had made a new friend. She was even happier that she had her new pink and white sock for the wedding tomorrow.

Anna went back inside to her room and finally drifted off to sleep again.

As soon as Anna woke up, she rushed out to the kitchen to tell her mom of her new friend Edgar and all the excitement of last night. She told her mom about the Magic Red Rock that Edgar had left in the backyard .

"Mom, it glows in the dark," Anna cried.

Anna's mom smiled. "That's wonderful, dear, but with all the dancing, sock stealing, glowing rocks, and far-away planets, how did you find your sock for the wedding?"

Anna replied with a smile. "It wasn't lost at all. Edgar is the Sock Stealer and he had stolen my sock and others too, but he comes back and returns them in a couple weeks. Don't worry mom, I taught Edgar a good lesson on stealing. I told him it was naughty and he had to ask from now on. So, now instead of stealing the socks, he will ask us if he can borrow or have them. Wasn't that a good lesson mom?"

Anna's mom smiled, and said; "Yes, Anna! I'm very proud of you for teaching your new friend right from wrong, you are a great friend!" Mom continued with a laugh and said; "A Sock Stealer - oops - I mean a Sock Borrower named Edgar, a Magic Red Rock and a wonderful lesson on stealing and borrowing. Ha ha, what a silly dream you had."

Chapter
Three

The
Magic Red Rock

A few days after the wedding, Anna and Hailie were sitting by her window looking out into the night sky. Hailie was spending the night with Anna. They were munching on a bedtime snack of peanut butter cookies, and dunking them in their glasses of milk. Anna was telling Hailie about the wedding. She told her friend how everyone had said she looked so pretty in her new pink dress with her matching socks. The wedding had been fun, she loved spreading, and tossing the pink rose petals everywhere. She wanted to throw them up in the air, but she wasn't allowed to do that. There had been a big party afterwards, but it hadn't been nearly as much fun as her party with Hailie.

"We DID have fun, didn't we?" responded Hailie.

Anna yawned. The moon was bright and the sky was full of stars. For a second, she thought she saw a shadow move behind her bed. She was holding the Magic Red Rock that Edgar had left behind.

Anna could see the twinkling red star that Edgar said was his home.

"*I miss Edgar,*" Anna thought.

"Hailie," Anna decided, "can you keep a secret?" When Hailie grinned and nodded, Anna told her all about Edgar and the missing socks.

"I think they come to my house too, said Hailie. When I need to sort out our socks, there always seems to be one or two missing. Wish I could meet Edgar," Hailie said sadly.

Then, all of a sudden, Ahhh-ha! Anna had an idea.

"C'mon, Hailie," she said, grabbing Hailie's hand and rushing outside to her backyard where she placed the Magic Red Rock in the grass. They waited, and waited, and waited. Nothing happened.

Anna pointed out Edgar's star. As she looked up to the bright red star, she thought about Edgar. With the moon shining bright and the sky filled with stars, Anna thought of her new friend and wondered how he was. The Magic Red Rock began to shake and jiggle. Then it went crackle, crackle, crack, crumpetty crack and pop-pop! It opened up like a cracked egg! Anna and Hailie jumped back quickly.

The girls peeked inside as it began to glisten and sparkle. They looked closer and they could see bursting curly sparkles coming out of the rock.

"*Ahhh…Magic!*" Anna said in amazement.

Anna stepped closer, looked back at her house, took Hailie's hand, and together, they hurried inside the Magic Red Rock.

Chapter
Four

The
Rock Tunnel

Whoosh! Whoosh! Whippet-Whap! went the Magic Red Rock. As soon as Anna and Hailie stepped inside, the rock closed. Anna and Hailie found themselves walking through a tunnel with some strange looking creatures all around. There were many different beings all busily going in many different directions.

"This is fun!" exclaimed Hailie.

There were creatures coming and going; walking past them, behind them and beside them. Some were wide and tall, others were short and skinny. Some had funny noses and ears. One had six arms with six mismatched mittens on each hand. There was another creature that had four legs with a different shoe on each foot. One had a very, very long neck that was striped and had bunches of multi-colored scarves wrapped around it. Another looked like a tiger with long floppy ears, big eyes, hands and feet with three fingers and toes! Some of the creatures looked a lot like Anna and Hailie, but none looked exactly like the people they knew.

Off the main tunnel that the girls were walking down were side tunnels leading to other planets. Anna pointed to a sign that said, 'This way to the planet of Stolen Keys.'

"I bet that's where my dad's keys all go," giggled Hailie.

"This way to the planet of Stolen Mittens" announced another sign.

I wonder if they are all borrowed shoes, keys, and mittens just like my socks? Don't they know it is wrong to steal? Anna

27

and Hailie scooted to the side of the tunnel as a huge blue centipede came down the tunnel shouting, "Make Way, Make Way!"

Hailie said, "He probably needs to shout like that because he takes up the whole tunnel!" Anna tried to count his bare feet as he went by, but she lost count. She snickered, thinking it was a good thing *he* wasn't a sock stealer, oh, sock borrower, now. Anna smiled.

Chapter
Five

Fuzzawalla
World

Anna and Hailie finally came to a sign that read, "This way to the home of the Fuzzawallas!" As Anna turned into the tunnel, she saw beings that looked a lot like Edgar, but they were all different colors. Anna began to walk a little faster.

"Hurry up, Hailie! I want to see Edgar's world!"

They came to a small green and yellow painted door with a sign made out of socks saying, "Welcome to the home of the Fuzzawallas!"

Anna was excited as she reached for the door knob.... "Creak" went the door as it opened. Hailie and Anna slowly crept inside.

Inside, there were Fuzzawallas everywhere. They were so many different colors that it looked like a rainbow had exploded! Some were riding bikes with two big wobbly tires in the front, and one in the back. Others were walking on tall striped stilts. One mom Fuzzawalla was pushing a buggy with a baby Fuzzawalla in it. There were young and old Fuzzawallas everywhere.

Anna turned, and right beside her was an orange Fuzzawalla. She had long orange and green hair and a big bushy orange and purple tail that lay over her shoulder.

"Hello, welcome!" The orange Fuzzawalla said to Anna and Hailie.

"Hello, who are you?" Anna said.

"My name is Lulu." Anna smiled and looked down

at Lulu's foot; she was wearing Anna's yellow sock.

Lulu said, "Thank you for all the socks. Edgar told everyone how nice you were, and he shared all the socks you gave him. He also taught us the difference between stealing and borrowing!

Anna smiled, "You are welcome and I'm glad he taught everyone the lesson. This is my very best friend, Hailie."

Anna was amazed as she looked around. It looked just like a city. Lulu asked the girls if they wanted to see Edgar. Anna nodded yes and away they went.

They walked through the city. There were tall, short, thick and thin sock buildings everywhere. Each building was shaped like a sock, and the doors were in the toes. Several of the buildings were shaped like a pair of socks with windows spiraling up the sides. They saw a couple that looked like knee-sock buildings. "Sock-scrapers!" giggled Anna. Anna and Hailie looked at each other and laughed at the giant sock buildings with doors in the toes.

Instead of streets, there were walkways with buildings on both sides. There were no cars like on earth, and no smelly pollution in the air. In fact, the air smelled super fresh and clean.

Lulu escorted them by a pink and orange sock building with lots of windows going up the tall part of the sock. The windows were open and Anna smelled something baking. Anna knew that smell! So, did Hailie. It smelled like Anna's Grandma Pidgie's peanut butter cookies.

Awesome, Anna thought.

"I'm hungry for some cookies," said Hailie. "I wish we'd brought some with us!"

After they walked through the town, and down through a grassy area, they reached a cluster of mushroom shaped houses. Almost the same idea as Anna's neighborhood, except that these houses were made of hollowed-out rock and shaped like mushrooms.

"This is my home," pointed Lulu, as they walked by a purple mushroom house with a door shaped like a sock."

Anna smiled, thinking how strange it would seem to her to live in a house made out of stone, shaped like a mushroom and with a sock-shaped door. *I'd have to be very careful not to trip going in*, she thought. *Everyone is different and what is regular for me might seem very strange to someone else, especially that ginormous centipede*, she thought.

They continued on their journey to find Edgar. As they walked over a small hill, the town and houses disappeared out of sight.

Chapter
Six

What's a Sock Eater?

Lulu said, "We have to be careful that we don't wake the Sock Eaters; they will eat your socks right off your feet!"

"Oh, my!" Anna gasped and continued, "What's a Sock Eater?"

"Yikers zikers!" said Hailie. Then in a whispered voice Hailie asked, "What are they and why do they eat socks? I wouldn't think stinky socks would taste very good!"

Lulu giggled quietly and whispered, "A long time ago some *other* Fuzzawallas went to Earth to steal socks. While they were there, they ate some peanut butter cookies and used the stolen socks as napkins. That left a trace of cookie on the socks. On their way back to our home, they smelled the peanut butter cookie crumbs on the socks and tried to eat the crumbs. They ended up eating holes in the socks instead. Those *other* Fuzzawallas have never stopped eating peanut butter cookies or socks ever since that day. That is why we don't play with them."

Anna laughed at the story and said, "Do they think our socks smell like peanut butter cookies?"

"What has that got to do with playing with them?" asked Hailie.

"Would *you* want to play with someone who eats your socks?" asked Anna. "I wouldn't."

Then they all laughed at the silly Sock Eating Fuzzawallas who thought socks smelled like peanut butter cookies.

The three girls came to a bridge made of colorful rocks. There were metallic purple rocks that smelled like grapes and sparkly green rocks that smelled like limes. There were shiny red rocks that smelled like apples and lemony-smelling yellow ones.

"Let's rest," said Lulu and they all sat down next to each other. Lulu took off her mismatched socks and put her feet in the stream to cool down. Anna did too. Hailie sat cross-legged and leaned back on her hands as she looked around.

As they sat there cooling their feet, Anna saw something in the water. As she looked closer, she could not believe her eyes. It looked just like a horse, but it was swimming like a fish in the water.

"Hailie! Look!" she said pointing into the water.

It had four legs, a head, four ears, two eyes, a very long triple braided tail and fish fins, and it swam in the water. It looked so funny. Both girls started to laugh.

In a flash, many more of the swimming horses appeared. They were whistling and jumping in and out of the water.

Lulu laughed with Anna and Hailie before telling them that they were Pea-giggles and would give the Fuzzawallas rides.

Anna was excited and jumped up and said, "Can we ride one now?"

"Please?" asked Hailie.

Just as Hailie said that, a purple and white Pea-giggle with a yellow tail came up to her and bent down so she could get on to go for a ride. Anna and Lulu jumped on a white and red Pea-giggle together. When they all reached the bottom of Feggimittel Hill, the Pea-giggles stopped and looked up the hill.

"Shhh!" said Lulu, and then she whispered in Anna's ear, "I think it's a Sock Eater. Shhh!"

Lulu, Hailie and Anna quietly got down, smiled at the Pea-giggles, and whispered, "Thank you." They crept over to the grass, put their socks back on and started walking up Feggimittel Hill. As they got closer, there on the top stood a Sock Eater, with a half-munched sock dangling out of his mouth.

"Ohhh no!" shouted Lulu, "run as fast as you can!"

They all started running back to the water. They hoped the Pea-giggle's would still be there to help them

41

escape the Sock Eater. When they reached the water, the Pea-giggles were nowhere in sight, but neither was the Sock Eater.

"Let's rest for a minute, I don't think he followed us," Lulu said as she sat down in the grass and took off her socks again.

Anna sat down and took off her socks too. When all of a sudden, whip, snap, grab, went the Sock Eater. He had run up behind the girls and stolen Anna's sock. Quick as a flash, the Sock Eater was out of sight.

"Oh no!" shouted Anna, "he stole my sock!

"We better go find Edgar. He will know what to do," said Lulu. Off they went again, up Feggimittel Hill.

Chapter
Seven

Looking for Edgar

When they reached the top of Feggimittel Hill, Anna and Hailie were amazed. "Wow! What are those?" Anna asked as she pointed toward the sky.

"They are Feggimittels, kind of like your flowers, but ours float in a cloud," Lulu explained with a smile.

Both girls looked around. There were Feggimittels of all colors, shapes, and sizes floating in the air. Some looked like red daffodils and others looked like blue daisies. Anna saw one that looked like a lilac flower except that it was orange. *An orange lilac*, thought Anna. *How funny!* She sniffed in. It smelled like orange-juicy lilacs!

Hailie noticed one with three big floppy Green petals and a big Orange middle with what looked like two black eyes and a big blue smile.

They weren't in the ground like the flowers on Earth. No, not these Feggimittels, they were floating up in the air, in a big cloud.

Hailie spun around, arms spread wide as she looked all around at the Feggimittels. One floated down right about Hailie's nose. She reached up to touch it and heard the most beautiful sound. It was as if someone strummed a harp.

"Anna," Hailie exclaimed. "They sound like wind chimes, only better!"

Anna chuckled as she walked under them floating above her in the sky.

The orange lilac one bent down, smiled, and winked at Anna.

Wow! Floating Feggimittels that smile and wink, Anna thought. She liked the way it smelled too, like orange juice and lilacs!

Lulu told the girls that they had to keep going over the hill to Treggle Valley to find Edgar. Anna nodded her head and away they all went.

When they arrived at the valley, the girls noticed some big trees. At least they looked sort of like trees, but these trees were different. They were big, with colored rocks hanging on them. Not with branches and leaves on top. These had tree roots waving about in the air. Down near the ground, were branches and round, shiny green leaves. They had eyes and mouths too.

Whoever had seen an upside-down tree that grew rocks instead of an apple or an orange or a banana? Anna thought.

"Hello, Lulu," one Treggle said.

"This is the sock girl. Her name is Anna, and this is her best friend, Hailie," Lulu told the Treggle that had red rocks dangling on his upside down roots.

"Hello, Anna and Hailie," said the Treggle.

Anna was so excited. She started to giggle and said, "I can't believe it. A talking tree, too."

The red Treggle looked at Anna and said in a huffy tone, "Hum! We are not trees, I'll thank you!"

46

"Oh my! I'm sorry, Sir. You look sort of like the trees on my planet," Anna said.

"Well, all right then, as long as you don't call us trees, because we are Treggles - not trees, and we live on Fuzzawalla World, not Earth World," declared the red Treggle. "Not every place is the same, you know," he said sternly.

"Very nice to meet you, Mr. Red Treggle," Anna said with a smile as the Treggle reached out a root and shook Anna's hand. "I need to remember that just because the way things are here isn't the same as at home, they are no better or worse, just different." Hailie nodded and smiled in agreement.

"That is an important lesson to learn," smiled the Red Treggle. "I grow the Magic Red Rocks."

Anna turned and looked behind the red Treggle. Then she noticed there were also green and blue Treggles coming toward them.

"We all grow rocks for special things," said Mr. Green Treggle. "My rocks help the Fuzzawallas bounce high into the air."

"Blue is for sad Fuzzawallas. My blue rocks make them happy," said Mr. Blue Treggle.

Anna and Hailie were excited to meet and learn of so many different things in Fuzzawalla World. Anna was eager to find her new friend, Edgar, so he could get her sock back from the Sock Eater before he ate the toe right out of it.

Lulu asked Mr. Red Treggle if he had seen Edgar. He told her that Edgar had just left and was chasing a

Sock Eater who had a sock in his hand.

Anna declared, "That must be my sock!" Hailie nodded her head in agreement.

Mr. Green Treggle said, "Edgar is headed to the Magic Red Rock at the edge of town." Then he continued, "If you would like, we can give you a ride there. Hop on."

"Great!" said Lulu as she climbed up Mr. Red Treggle and sat on a root. Then Anna climbed up on a blue Treggle while Hailie hoisted herself on a low curved root offered by a Purple Treggle, and away they went.

Chapter Eight

Finally Edgar

When they reached town, Edgar was standing by the Magic Red Rock.

"Wait!" shouted Anna, "a Sock Eater stole my sock."

Edgar told Anna the Sock Eater had leapt into the Magic Red Rock and was gone. Edgar looked over at Hailie then Anna introduced Hailie and Edgar to each other.

"Now, what am I going to do?" said Anna with a sad voice, "I have to go home now or my mom will be worried."

Lulu bent down, took off one of her socks, handed it to Anna, and then gave her a goodbye hug. She told Anna she could borrow her sock until they caught the Sock Eater and could get her sock back. Anna smiled and gave Lulu a hug too and said, "Thank you."

Edgar told Anna she could visit any time. "Just put the Magic Red Rock in the moonlight and think of me," Edgar said. "Hailie, please keep our secret. Just imagine if everyone on your world knew about Fuzzawalla World."

"No one would believe me, anyway!" Hailie promised. Then she turned around with a big wave and a smile and Jiggity-jig, clip-pity, clap-pity! In the Magic Red Rock she and Anna went. They saw all the strange beings on their way home, the key monster, the mitten critter, and the four-legged guy. Soon the girls arrived in Anna's backyard. They saw Willie, Anna's own four-legged critter sitting there, swishing his tail and licking his front paw.

The next morning Anna and Hailie ran into the kitchen, "Mom, Mom!" Anna shouted, "the Magic Red Rock that Edgar left behind really IS magic. Hailie and I used it to get to Fuzzawalla World. They have a city made of colorful rock buildings with sock curtains and sock doors. We rode Pea-giggles and I talked to a Treggle, and they even had floating Feggimittels.

"Really?" Anna's mom said, "How did you get to this planet of Fuzzawalla's who steal socks oops! I mean borrow socks with just a silly old rock?"

"Oh Mom, it's not just a silly old rock."

"It's a Magic Red Rock," added Hailie before she remembered her promise.

Anna continued, "I put it in the grass in the back-yard and the moonlight shone on it, and it opened up. We stepped inside and went to the Planet of the Fuzzawallas. On the way there, we saw other creatures. One had six long arms and hands and each hand had a different mitten. Another one had four legs and four shoes on each foot. Oh, and we made a new Fuzzawalla friend, Lulu and she's orange!"

Anna's mom laughed and looked down at Anna's feet, "How did you get different socks on?" she asked.

"Oh yes, well you see, a Sock Eater stole one of my socks and Lulu loaned me one of hers until I can go back and find the Sock Eater who stole my sock and get it back," Anna explained.

"Well, Anna , maybe your Grandma Pidgie can go

with you to where the Fuzzawallas live next time and help you rescue your sock from that Sock Eating creature," she said with a loud laugh. Then she continued, "Grandma is coming tomorrow to stay for a week."

"Yeah!" Anna shouted, "Grandma Pidgie!"

"Anna, I am glad you have such a wonderful imagination. I love your Magic Red Rock adventures," Anna's Mom said with a giggle and a smile. "And isn't it funny that you and Hailie had such similar dreams?"

Chapter
Nine

Grandma
Pidgie's Visit

As soon as the school bell rang, Anna hurried out of her classroom door to the school buses. She was excited because Grandma Pidgie was coming today. Anna wanted to have her room all ready when her grandma arrived.

When the school bus drove up to Anna's house, she rushed off the bus and ran inside her house. She threw down her backpack and hurried to her room. She made her bed, folded a blanket and fluffed her pillow. She dusted off her dresser, shoved some toys under her bed and into her toy box too. She looked around her room, "Ahhh! Almost done," she said. Then she began to set the table for a tea party.

Anna went to the hallway closet and took out a small tablecloth that fit the table in her room. She spread the cloth out smoothly, and then she placed her favorite tea set on the table. It was her favorite because her Grandma Pidgie went all the way to Nashville, Tennessee and brought it back for her.

One last thing, Anna thought. She took two of her furry friends off her bed and placed them in two empty chairs around her table. "There, now I'm ready," she said.

Knock! Knock! Anna raced to the door. "Grandma! Grandma!" she roared with excitement.

"Hello, my Pirate Princess Anna," Grandma Pidgie said. Grandma Pidgie called Anna 'Pirate Princess' because she loved to go on great adventures and find treasures and magical things. Grandma always told Anna that she had a very active imagination.

"I'm happy you are here. Do you want to have a tea party?" Anna asked as she grabbed her Grandma's hand and began pulling her toward her room.

"I would love to have a tea party with you," Grandma said. "Who is coming?"

"Polly and Raisin," Anna replied.

"Wonderful. I will be right there," Grandma said.

Within minutes of Grandma Pidgie's arrival, they were having a tea party. Anna had invited Polly, the lamb, and Raisin, the walrus, to join them.

"Grandma, I have some different friends too. They are Fuzzawallas and they come from another planet," Anna explained.

"I had an unusual little friend when I was your age too," Grandma Pidgie said.

"Really? Was your friend from another planet? Did he steal your socks?"

"Why, yes," Grandma said with a surprised look.

"What was his name?" Anna asked.

"My friend's name was Edgar. Do you know Edgar?"

Anna squealed with excitement while waving her hands in the air.

"When I was a little girl, Edgar visited me right in this very room," Grandma told Anna. "I have been

60

making socks for him and his little furry friends. But as I got older I never saw him again," she said sadly.

"Edgar is a Fuzzawalla. Hailie and I went to visit his planet," said Anna. "Would you like to go see Edgar too, Grandma?"

"Yes!" Grandma said with a big smile as she waved her hands in the air too.

Anna went to her sock drawer and took out the Magic Red Rock that Edgar had left behind the first time he had visited her room. She held it out and showed it to Grandma Pidgie.

Chapter
Ten

Fuzzawalla Land

Later that evening, Anna and her grandma went to the backyard and put the rock in the grass under the moonlight. Anna stepped back and told her grandma to step back too.

"You have to think about Edgar now, Grandma. That is what makes the magic work."

Then she waited. Sure enough, in just a couple minutes the rock began to shake and jiggle. And it went crackle, crackle, crack, crumpetty crack and poppity pop!

Grandma Pidgie could not believe what she was seeing. "Oh my word!" she said. But there it was the Magic Red Rock opening up right in Anna's backyard. Grandma Pidgie said in amazement, "It's a real Magic Red Rock!"

The Magic Red Rock began to glisten and sparkle. And, just like before, there was a bursting of curly sparkles coming from inside it.

"It's magic!" Anna said with excitement!

Anna took hold of Grandma Pidgie's hand. "Let's go, Grandma." and they stepped into the Magic Red Rock together. Whoosh! Whoosh! Whippet- whap! went the Magic Red Rock once again.

As they began walking in the Magic Red Rock tunnel, Anna told Grandma, "I've got to warn you, it's kind of strange in here. The creatures are nice, just funny looking."

Soon they were passing all kinds of different

creatures and lots of rock tunnels that led to different planets. Anna pointed out the same signs she saw from before when she came to visit Edgar. She pointed to a sign that read *"This way to the Planet of Stolen Keys."* Then she pointed to another one, *"This way to the Planet of Stolen Mittens."*

Anna said, "These creatures steal things. Maybe I should teach them the difference between stealing and borrowing too!"

Grandma couldn't believe it; she was walking inside a Magic Red Rock. She was seeing all sorts of different looking creatures, and learning what really happens to all of everyone's lost and or stolen things.

"Look!" Anna pointed at a sign that read, *"This way to the Planet of the Fuzzawallas."*

As they turned the corner, right in front of them was the sign and door to Fuzzawalla World. Grandma said, "Anna, you were right."

Anna and her grandma opened the door and walked inside. It was just like Anna said. There were Fuzzawallas everywhere!

Chapter
Eleven

Whose Manners?

Lulu heard the Magic Red Rock's crackle and she knew Anna was coming, but she didn't know Anna was bringing someone with her again. "Hello, Anna. Who is this?" Lulu asked.

"This is my Grandma Pidgie. She knew Edgar when she was little," Anna explained.

"We are so glad you are here," Lulu continued, "The Sock Eater that stole your sock came back and we caught him. Edgar and the Sock Eater are in the Valley of Treggles right now."

"Oh, no, we'd better get to Treggle Valley right away!" Anna exclaimed.

"Yes, we better hurry," Lulu agreed.

So Anna, Lulu, and Grandma Pidgie rushed to Treggle Valley to find Edgar and the Sock Eater.

They walked through the city of rock buildings just like Anna explained to her grandma. They passed the funny shaped mushroom houses. Then they were at the rock bridge where the Pea-giggles lived. They traveled to Feggimittel Hill where the floating Feggimittels dangled from the sky.

Grandma Pidgie could not believe her eyes. She gasped and smiled all at once. Anna and Lulu just giggled.

"We'd better hurry," Lulu reminded. And they began to walk faster toward Treggle Valley to find Edgar and the Sock Eater.

As they passed by Feggimittel Hill, Grandma reached out and touched some dangling Feggimittels, they danced in the air to the pretty sounds of harp music. Around and around, up and down bobbing their heads side to side and up and down they danced. Grandma was astonished at all she saw.

Finally, they reached Treggle Valley. There stood two huge Treggles right in front of the gate into the valley.

"Who goes there?" The Green Treggle said, as he moved his biggest root in front of Lulu, Grandma and Anna.

"It's me, Lulu, Mr. Green." Lulu continued, "I brought Anna and Grandma Pidgie. We must go inside the valley right away, step aside."

"Nope, you can't go inside!" said Mr. Green Treggle.

"Oh, but you *have* to let us in!" Lulu exclaimed. "It was Anna's sock that was stolen," Lulu continued to plead.

"Oh, let us pass, Mr. Green Treggle. We need to get to Edgar!" Anna stamped her foot as she insisted the Treggle let them through.

"No! I told you once. Now go away!" said Mr. Green Treggle.

Grandma Pidgie said in a nice voice, "Mr. Green Treggle, would you 'please' allow us to pass? That is Anna's sock that was stolen."

Mr. Green Treggle looked at Grandma, Anna and

Lulu, and then replied, "Well, I sure will. Do you know why I am letting you pass now?"

Lulu shook her head and shrugged. Anna thought about it and said, "Because Grandma Pidgie said, 'please'?"

The Treggle's grumpy look turned to a big smile as he nodded. "Always remember that manners are important wherever you go! Now, you'd best hurry."

Chapter Twelve

Being Different is a Good Thing

Grandma, Anna and Lulu rushed into Treggle Valley. They found Edgar and the Sock Eating Fuzzawalla both standing there quarrelling. The Sock Eating Fuzzawalla looked a lot like Edgar, but his tail was short and furry, not a puffball like what Edgar and Lulu had.

Grandma Pidgie listened to them for a minute and then she knew just what to do. Grandma walked over to them. She stepped in-between them and said, "Now, shush, shush, what's going on here?"

Edgar looked at Grandma Pidgie and said, "This Sock Eater stole Anna's sock. We don't like Sock Eating Fuzzawallas. They live on the other side of our planet and they look different and eat holes in socks."

Grandma Pidgie gave Edgar a grumpy look. "There are many different looking people on planet Earth where we come from, but everyone tries to get along. We are different colors and we all eat different foods just like

Fuzzawallas do and we have different cultures and houses and names, but it is always better to try to get along, and celebrate the differences, not fight.

"But they steal our socks then eat holes in them. They sneak our peanut butter cookies too," said Lulu. They don't even ask. They are the worst kind of Fuzzawallas."

Anna spoke up and said, "Wait a minute. You Fuzzawallas stole our socks too, until I taught you the difference between stealing and asking to borrow things, didn't you?"

Edgar and Lulu both looked at each other and nodded their heads in agreement with Anna.

Anna continued, "Edgar and Lulu, just because someone is different from you, doesn't mean they are a bad person. Oops, I mean a bad Fuzzawalla. You can teach the lesson I taught you to the Sock Eaters too, Edgar! Then all the sock stealing and cookie stealing might stop, if they knew it was naughty.

The Sock Eater took off the sock he had stolen from Anna and handed it back to her. He looked at Anna and said, "I'm sorry. I just wanted to play and have friends too. Please forgive me for stealing your sock."

Anna took her sock and said thank you to the different looking Fuzzawalla that was a Sock Eater. She then asked him, "What is your name?"

"I'm Marvin" he said.

Anna took Marvin by the hand, then reached out and took Edgar's hand as well, and said, "I'm not mad at Marvin anymore. He didn't even eat a hole in my sock either! Let's all be friends because everyone is different and that's okay." Then Anna joined Marvin's and Edgar's hands and said, "Shake hands and be friends."

Marvin and Edgar looked at each other. They shook hands. Then Lulu gave Marvin a hug and everyone smiled.

"Hip Hip Hooray! Hip Hip Hooray!" Everyone roared as they all took turns shaking hands with Marvin and even each other.

Chapter
Thirteen

Clippity clap-
Zippity zap!

Grandma Pidgie looked at her watch and said to Anna, "We'd better hurry up and get back home. It's almost morning on Earth."

The five of them rushed through Treggle Valley, over Feggimittel Hill, onto the rock bridge where the Pea-giggles lived. They passed the mushroom houses and the city. They rushed all the way back to the Magic Red Rock at the edge of Fuzzawalla town.

Clip-pity! Clap-pity! They all stepped into the Magic Red Rock and began their journey back to Earth - Grandma Pidgie, Anna, Edgar, Marvin and Lulu. Soon they were all walking out of the Magic Red Rock into Anna's backyard.

"Shhh!" Anna said to Marvin, Edgar and Lulu, with a quiet voice and her finger pressed against her lips, "Don't wake my mother. She thinks I *dream* about you Fuzzawallas. She doesn't believe you guys are real. I don't want to scare her."

So they all tiptoed into Anna's room.

Grandma went into the guest room and returned with a big bag of knitted socks. "Here are all the socks I have made for you and all your friends," she said. "I've always hoped to see you again, Edgar. I've been working on these for years, just in case." The bag was so big and full she could hardly carry it. Edgar, Marvin and Lulu smiled at Grandma Pidgie.

"What a socksational gift," Edgar said with a snort. Then everyone snorted, giggled and repeated, "SOCKSATIONAL!"

"Before you go, would you like some peanut butter cookies and tea?" Anna asked.

"Oh, yes, please," Marvin said while rubbing his tummy, licking his lips, wagging his tail up and down and round and round and nodding his head all at the same time.

They all sat down at Anna's play table in her room. The five of them laughed quietly, ate peanut butter cookies, and drank tea (which was really juice). Soon it was time for the Fuzzawallas to go back to their glowing red planet.

Grandma Pidgie, Anna and the three Fuzzawallas tiptoed outside to the Magic Red Rock. Edgar invited Grandma Pidgie and Anna to come back and visit. Marvin and Lulu nodded their heads and smiled. Then Marvin said, "And you can bring some peanut butter cookies too." Everyone laughed.

"We would love to visit you Fuzzawallas again," said Grandma Pidgie.

Edgar, Marvin and Lulu all took a corner of the big bag of knitted socks with one hand and with the other, they waved good-bye as they stepped into the Magic Red Rock and went home to their world.

The next morning, Anna and Grandma Pidgie were whispering at the kitchen table.

"Should we tell her?" Grandma Pidgie whispered to Anna.

"No! She thinks I have silly dreams about the Fuzzawallas and the Magic Red Rock," Anna replied softly. Anna and her grandma just smiled at each other as Mom walked into the kitchen.

"Good morning, Mom" Anna said.

"Did you have any more of your amazingly awesome silly dreams, Anna?" Mom asked.

"No dreams!" Anna replied, with a smile, a giggle, and a wink at Grandma Pidgie.

Chapter
Fourteen

The
Invitation

It was a few days after Anna and Grandma Pidgie had returned from Fuzzawalla Land. They had been having lots of fun playing together and enjoying their visit. One night, Anna went to bed early because she and her grandma had played extra hard that day and she was very tired.

Knock! Knock!

Anna woke up when she heard knocking. She thought someone was knocking on her bedroom door.

Knock! Knock!

"Who's there?" whispered Anna. Awake now, Anna realized the knocking was at her bedroom window.

"Anna, it's me, Lulu."

"What are you doing here? It's late." Anna said, with a yawn and a stretch.

"We want you and Grandma to come to Fuzzawalla World," Lulu said, "We have a surprise."

Grandma heard voices coming from Anna's room. She went to see whom Anna was talking with. She cracked open the bedroom door and saw the girls.

"Shhh! Anna and Lulu, you will wake Anna's Mom," Grandma whispered.

"The Fuzzawallas have a surprise for us, Grandma. May we go and see what it is?" Anna asked.

"Okay but we had better hurry before your Mom wakes up," Grandma said as she ran to get dressed.

Grandma was dressed in the wink of an eye.

"Are you girls ready?" Grandma asked. Grandma and Anna were both excited to find out what the surprise was.

Lulu put her Magic Red Rock in the backyard under the moonlight and, as usual, thought of her home. Crumple! Crack! Jiggity-jig went the rock.

Chapter
Fifteen

Wait for Me!

Just as the rock opened, Anna's mom came rushing out the back door into the yard. "Anna! Wait!" she yelled, but it was too late. Anna, Grandma and Lulu had vanished into the Magic Red Rock which then shrank back into an ordinary-looking sparkling red rock.

"Oh, no! Where did they go?" Anna's mom cried. "Who was that little, fuzzy creature?"

She looked at the Magic Red Rock on the ground. *It was a plain old red rock, how could they have jumped into it? Maybe I can open the rock and follow them,* Anna's mom thought

First, she tapped the rock on the ground, but nothing happened. Then she tapped the rock on the fence, and the porch and still nothing happened. She even tried rubbing it and nothing happened. Then she put the rock back on the ground where the moonlight shone down on it and she began to think of Anna, Grandma and the little fuzzy orange creature. All at once, the rock began to make noises and it grew larger and larger and larger.

Crumple! Crack! Jiggity-jig!

"Oh my goodness!" she shouted. The rock opened up, and she heard voices coming from inside the rock. She stepped closer to look into the rock and... Whoosh! Clang! Jangle! Into the Magic Red Rock she went. She was so surprised she could not believe her own eyes. It was just as Anna said.

I thought Anna was having silly dreams. Now I know she was not dreaming, Mom thought, as she kept walking and seeing all the creatures and signs to different planets that Anna had told her all about.

Soon Mom saw an open door and two little fuzzy creatures. "Hello, Welcome to Fuzzawalla World," said one of the creatures.

"Hello, who are you?" Mom asked.

"My name is Edgar and this is my friend Marvin. We are Anna and Grandma Pidgie's good friends. We are having a surprise parade for them. Anna and Grandma taught us the difference between stealing and asking to borrow something. And, they taught us it's okay to be friends with people who are different from you or I. They gave us some pretty socksational socks and we want to thank them by giving them a parade.

"It is so nice to finally meet you! When you were a little girl, you had that green dresser with the sticky drawers. We weren't strong enough to open them. You always put your socks away" continued Edgar, "before we could even get near them! You were such a neat little girl!"

"When Anna was little, I sanded the drawers down

92

so that I could use it in Anna's room. It is easier to open now, and it was quiet for a while, but it makes a terrible scrreeech now, when she opens it."

"I know," laughed Edgar.

"Would you like to help us get ready for the parade?" asked Marvin.

Anna's mom agreed with a big smile. Edgar and Marvin took her to the City.

Chapter Sixteen

Getting Ready!

"Oh my! This is just like Anna explained," Mom said.

Edgar winked at Marvin and they both giggled along side her. Soon they arrived where all the Fuzzawallas were preparing for the surprise parade.

"Where are Anna and her grandma?" asked Mom.

"Lulu took them over by the Treggle Forest. We didn't want them to see what was going on just yet. They will be here in a little while. Right now, we need to get ready!"

There were Fuzzawallas everywhere. Some were blowing colorful bubbles. Some were making flowers out of old socks. Others were building the big floats and painting them. Five Fuzzawallas were playing musical instruments. There was a guitar, a tambourine, a set of bongo drums, and a keyboard. There was even one Fuzzawalla playing a saxophone. There was music, dancing, singing and laughter everywhere.

Mom noticed little fuzzy balls bouncing all around. They looked a lot like the Fuzzawallas' tails! She stopped and listened as one Fuzzawalla was practicing a special song for Anna and Grandma.

"Ohhhh....we love peanut butter cookies...
And, we love SOCKSATIONAL socksssss...
socksssss... socksssss!
And we love Anna and Grandma Pidgie
because they are our friendssss... and they
super Rockkkk! Rockkkk! Rockkkk!
Oh yeah, we love peanut butter cookiessss...
and socksssss...socksssss...socksssss!"

97

Several small Fuzzawallas that eat socks or used to eat holes in them were busy weaving Feggimittels into musical wreathes for Anna and Grandma Pidgie to wear in their hair. A young purple Fuzzawalla handed Anna's Mom one made of green and white flowers. When she moved her head, the flowers chimed softly.

The smell of peanut butter cookies was wafting all over as Fuzzawalla Bakers were busy making enough cookies for everyone! There were plates and piles of cookies stacked on tables, chairs and benches!

What a sight this was to see!

Chapter
Seventeen

_____

Let the
Parade Begin!

At last, they were all ready. Someone said that Lulu and her friends were just over the hill.

Marvin shouted with excitement, "Everyone hide!"

Everyone was hiding in their places and waiting to surprise Grandma and Anna. Just as Anna and Grandma walked closer, all of the Fuzzawallas jumped out of their hiding spots and yelled, "SURPRISE!"

Everyone shouted, "Hooray for Anna! Hooray for Grandma Pidgie!" And, with one more big shout out of "Hip-Hip-Hooray!" the parade began and everyone started singing and dancing and the musicians began playing.

"Let the parade begin!" Edgar roared. "Here they come!"

Around the bend came all the floats. There was a large float that had a Treggle on it. Fuzzawallas were sitting on the roots and smiling and waving. There was a mushroom-shaped float with young and old Fuzzawallas blowing colorful bubbles to the crowds. Another float had Fuzzawallas tossing fuzzy balls off it until there were colorful fuzzy balls flying all over. Anna and Grandma started clapping their hands and dancing in the street, too.

Next came the biggest float of all. It looked just like a sock and the Fuzzawallas rolled it over to Grandma and Anna. The float was purple, red and yellow, with different sock flowers all over it.

"This is a special float we made just for the two of you," said Edgar and Marvin at the same time.

Anna and Grandma climbed up on the toe. Then they climbed up on the purple and green steps until they were able to sit on the very tip top. They were so delighted.

"Cool! A parade just for us," Grandma said.

The big sock float went down the street. Anna looked into the crowd. She was amazed at what she was seeing. Everyone looked so happy. Sock Eaters and Sock Borrowers stood side by side smiling. Then Anna got the biggest surprise of all!

There, on the sidewalk, stood her mom.

"Grandma, look!" Anna shouted and pointed toward her mom.

"Oh my word, Anna, It's your mom!"

Anna's mom waved. Grandma and Anna waved back with a big surprised smile.

The floats went by all the Fuzzawallas in town, past all the sock shops, peanut butter cookie stores and down to the park by the town square. There, up on a gaily decorated stage, Edgar and Marvin both gave speeches. The crowd clapped at their speeches. Then Edgar made Grandma Pidgie and Anna both honorary citizens of Fuzzawalla Land. He gave each of them a key shaped like a sock with a purple ribbon on the end of it! The Fuzzawalla chorus sang the song they'd been practicing and after a moment, everyone sang along together. Anna and Grandma Pidgie were given their Feggimittel Flower Wreaths and all the Fuzzawallas screamed for Anna to give a speech too.

"I don't really know what to say," Anna began. "I met Edgar when he was stealing my socks. We learned about things together. I taught him it isn't nice to steal. And, the Treggels taught me about being nice to people who do things differently than I might and saying please and thank you. We all learned about being nice. I'm glad that Edgar stole my socks and I am glad I could teach him a lesson on stealing and borrowing. I am really happy he taught everyone else, too. Isn't it fun how we all learned that we all are different in some way? And I'm glad I met Marvin and learned that it wasn't Hailie sneaking nibbles of my cookies! I love being here!"

Everyone cheered when she finished. Edgar helped Anna down from the stage. "I need to go find my Mom," Anna told Edgar before running off.

Chapter
Eighteen

Time to go Home

"Mom! What are you doing here?" Anna asked.

Mom said, "I heard voices in the backyard. Then I saw you, Grandma, and that little fuzzy orange creature hopping into your Magic Red Rock. I had to follow you. Anna, you were not having silly dreams at all. It really is a Magic Red Rock. There really is a planet for stolen, oops I mean borrowed socks and Fuzzawallas."

Everyone laughed, and Anna's mom joined in.

Edgar asked Mom if she would like to go for a walk. Mom was delighted and said, "Yes!"

Off they went to show Mom the city, mushroom houses, Pea-giggless, Feggimittel Hill and Treggle Valley. Anna's mom was so surprised, she could hardly believe it! After they visited all the places that Anna had told her about, it was time for Anna, Mom and Grandma to return to their own home back on earth. The three Fuzzawallas and the three Earthlings walked back to the Magic Red Rock at the edge of town.

Edgar said, "Come and visit any time."

"You may visit us any time, too," Anna's mom said. Then Anna, Mom and Grandma all stepped into the Magic Red Rock and headed back home. Soon they were walking into Anna's backyard again.

"Let's all get some rest before morning," Anna's Mom said. And they all went to their rooms to get some sleep. Anna snuggled down in her bed. She heard music

107

and realized she still had her Feggimittel Flowers on her head. She got up and put the wreath on top of her dresser, then jumped back into her bed. Anna smiled a sleepy smile as she fell asleep to soft music coming from the Feggimittels and she dreamed of the Fuzzawallas.

The next morning Anna and Grandma went to the kitchen for breakfast. There was Mom making Anna's favorite banana pancakes.

Anna's mom looked at both Anna and Grandma grinned then said, "I had the silliest dream ever last night."

Anna and Grandma looked at Mom and smiled and said, "Really? About what?"

Anna's mom told them all about the Magic Red Rock in the backyard. She told them about Edgar, Marvin and Lulu. She explained that she helped with a huge parade and that she had lots of fun.

Anna's mom continued, "Anna, you and Grandma were in the parade, now isn't that the silliest dream ever? It was so real. I really thought I was there." Then she sighed and went back to making her banana pancakes.

Anna and Grandma began to laugh. Anna looked at her mom and said, "What an amazingly awesome socksational dream you had, Mom. You have such adventurous dreams." And, then she giggled so hard syrup came out her nose as she ate her favorite banana pancakes. Grandma laughed and Mom just shook her head, rolled her eyes and sighed.

To learn more about Author Peggy
and her books visit:

www.AuthorPeggyG.com

and while you are there
you can request the special recipe
of Grandma Pidgie's
<u>Amazing Peanut Butter Cookies</u>
and Anna's favorite
<u>Banana Pancakes</u> too!

Peggy Grigowski began her writing career at the age of eight in 3rd grade. Her teacher at the time insisted she write a poem. She was not eager to do so and with her teacher's guidance and matter-of-fact attitude, Peggy wrote the poem. Winning 1st place in a school poetry contest is what sparked her to her writing career and love of words and creating stories.

Peggy's adventure of the Sock Stealer began with her oldest son; Anthony. He had lost one sock from a pair and at the age of three he blamed the lost sock on the green monster; thus began "The Sock Stealer."

Peggy enjoys storytelling and writing stories. She says that she can find inspiration everywhere, even in her backyard.

At present time Peggy is a licensed counselor in the state of Michigan, a seminar speaker and of course an author. She lives in Marshall with her husband; Gary and two dogs; Maggie and Polly. She has four children, and four grandchildren.

I like to draw, paint and create things.

I do this for others as a job.

But I enjoy doing it for myself and my friends too.

I believe life is too short to do something everyday that you don't love.

I also like to travel and stay up late watching old movies.

I once saw a UFO in the sky.

But later, I found out it did not come from outer space.

I also have two pet turtles, named Buddy and Elvis,

who follow me around the house.

You should always believe in yourself, and in your ideas.

You are just as good as anyone else.

And if you have something nice to share with others, do it.